BLACK WALL STREET
Archer ST 500
N Greenwood AV 100

Black Wall Street: The Spirit of Community

Identifiers: LCCN 2021906467
ISBN 978-1-7369406-0-0 (hardcover)
ISBN 978-1-7369406-1-7 (paperback)

Library of Congress Cataloging-in-Publication Data

First edition April 2021.

Made in the USA.

Houston, TX

www.ourhistorytold.com

This book is dedicated to the legacy of the entrepreneurs and dreamers of Black Wall Street. Although their story is often overlooked in history books, the impact of it continues to be felt beyond 1921.

Special thanks to my husband Onaje, children Saniya and Tariq, mom Loretta, sister Delisa, my guardian angels/my dads Willie and James, numerous family members and friends. You have individually and collectively encouraged me during this journey from creation to publication and I could not have done it without your support.

Have you ever heard of Black Wall Street? Have you ever thought about what Black Wall Street looked like? Well, let's travel back to the past and see what life was like at the corner of Greenwood and Archer, the hub of Black Wall Street.

In 1921, the Greenwood District was a beautiful and blooming neighborhood for Black residents in Tulsa, Oklahoma. In those days, it was common for Black and white people to live in separate areas because of Jim Crow laws. Jim Crow laws defined where Black people could live, where they could eat, where they could work, and what stores they could shop at.

So why the name Black Wall Street? Well, Wall Street was a popular area known for financial institutions and successful businesses focused on making money. Black Wall Street was similar to Wall Street, except for the fact that all the businesses were Black-owned and were supported by Black residents.

This Tulsa neighborhood became known as Black Wall Street after a visit from Booker T. Washington, educator and founder of the National Negro Business League. There were over 300 successful Black-owned businesses here and this impressed him. All of these businesses had been started, and were run, by Black business owners called entrepreneurs. Out of respect for their hard work, Booker T. Washington called the area Black Wall Street.

These businesses were supported by more than 10,000 Black residents living in the Greenwood District. It was once said that every dollar circulated among these businesses over 30 times before it was spent outside this community. Neighbors supported each other and this contributed to the success of Black Wall Street. Let's meet some of the people from the neighborhood.

In Greenwood, you could find a variety of Black-owned businesses, such as the ones developed by O.W. Gurley. Gurley was a wealthy landowner who purchased 40 acres of land that he used to start several businesses. The first was a rooming house that offered a safe space for migrants fleeing from other southern states. He also owned a parlor, a cafe, the Gurley Hotel, and the Vernon AME Church.

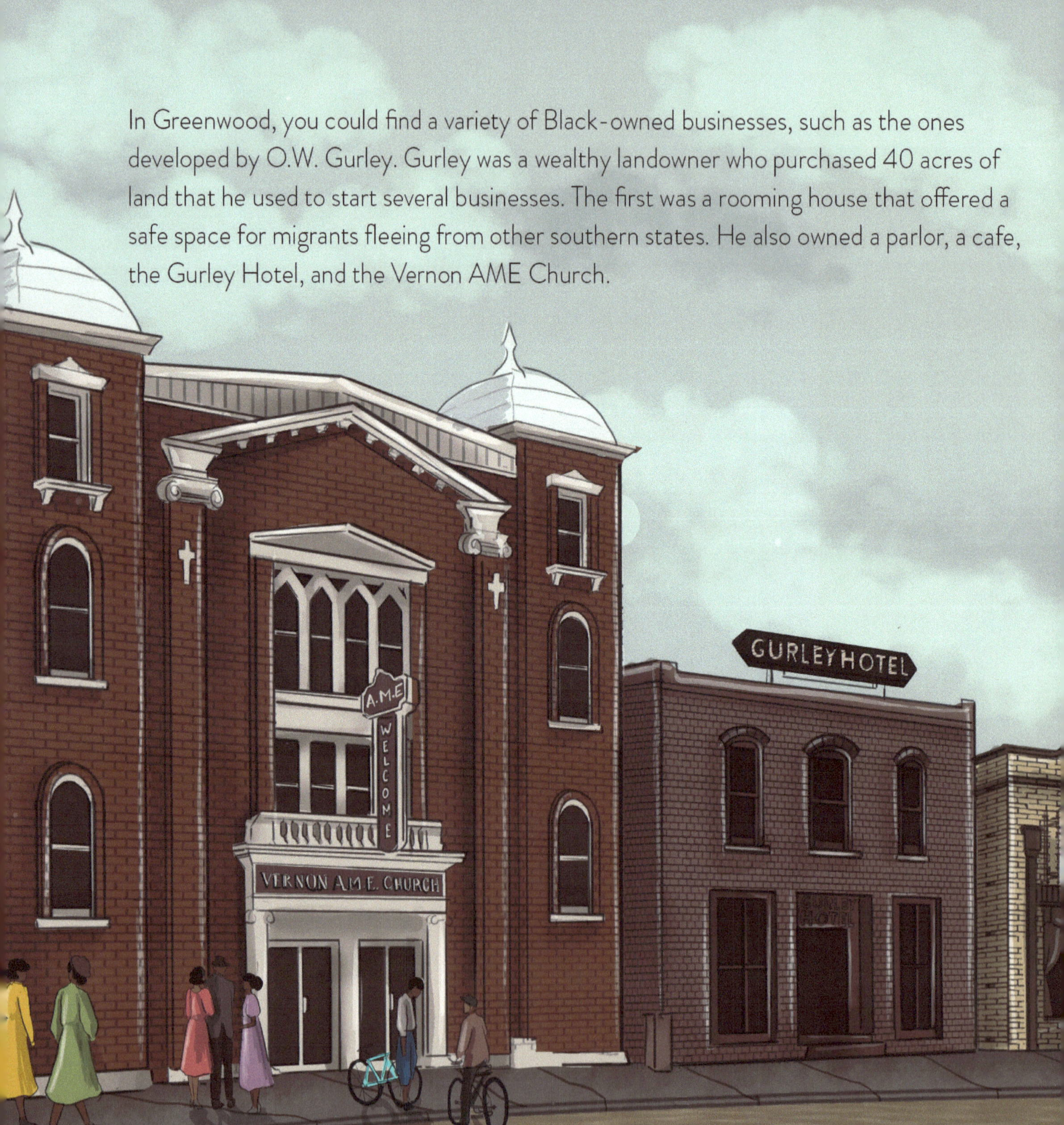

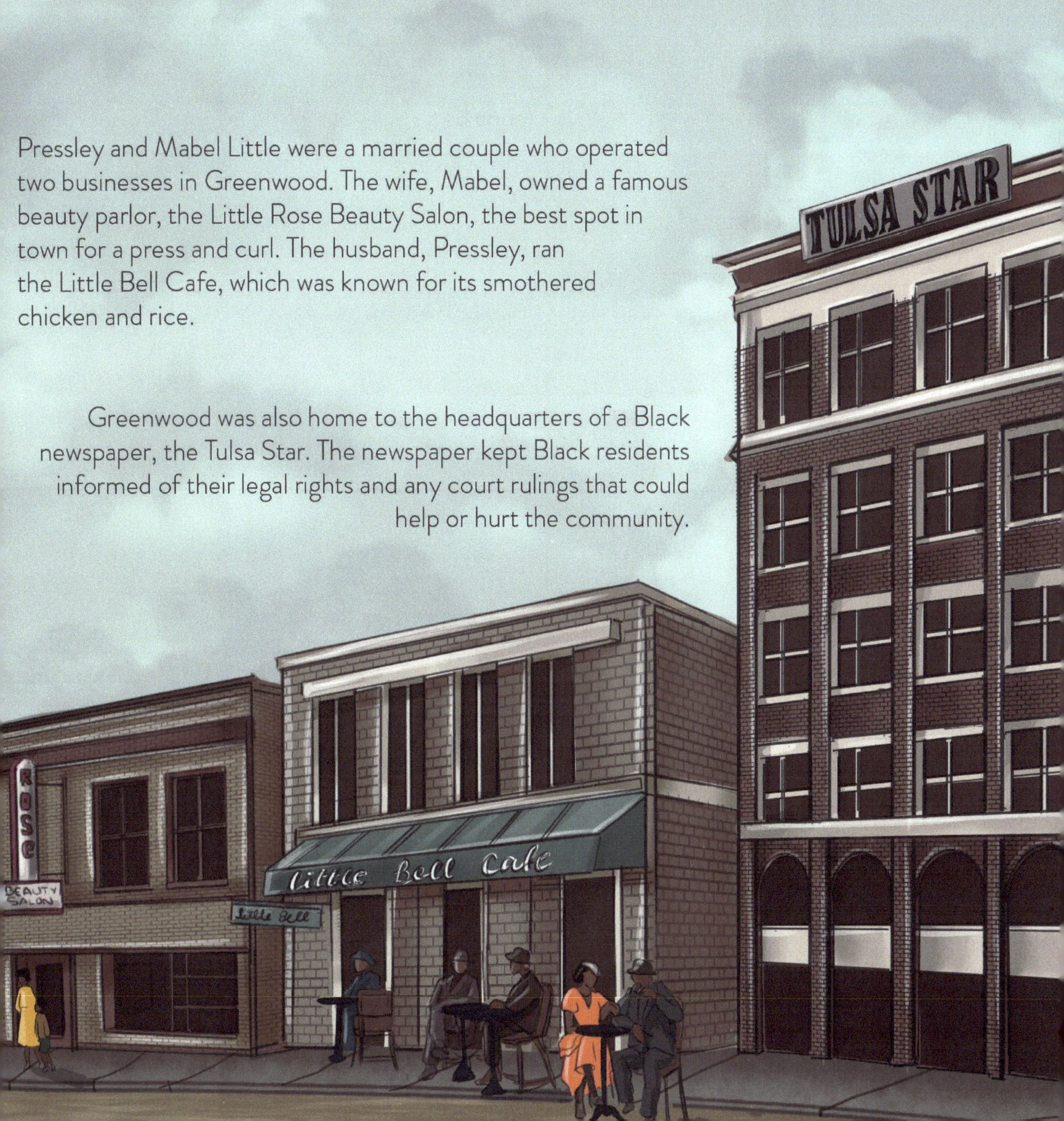

Pressley and Mabel Little were a married couple who operated two businesses in Greenwood. The wife, Mabel, owned a famous beauty parlor, the Little Rose Beauty Salon, the best spot in town for a press and curl. The husband, Pressley, ran the Little Bell Cafe, which was known for its smothered chicken and rice.

Greenwood was also home to the headquarters of a Black newspaper, the Tulsa Star. The newspaper kept Black residents informed of their legal rights and any court rulings that could help or hurt the community.

John and Loula Williams owned Dreamland Theatre, which featured piano music accompanied by silent movies and live entertainment. With over 700 seats, it was the entertainment hub of the area.

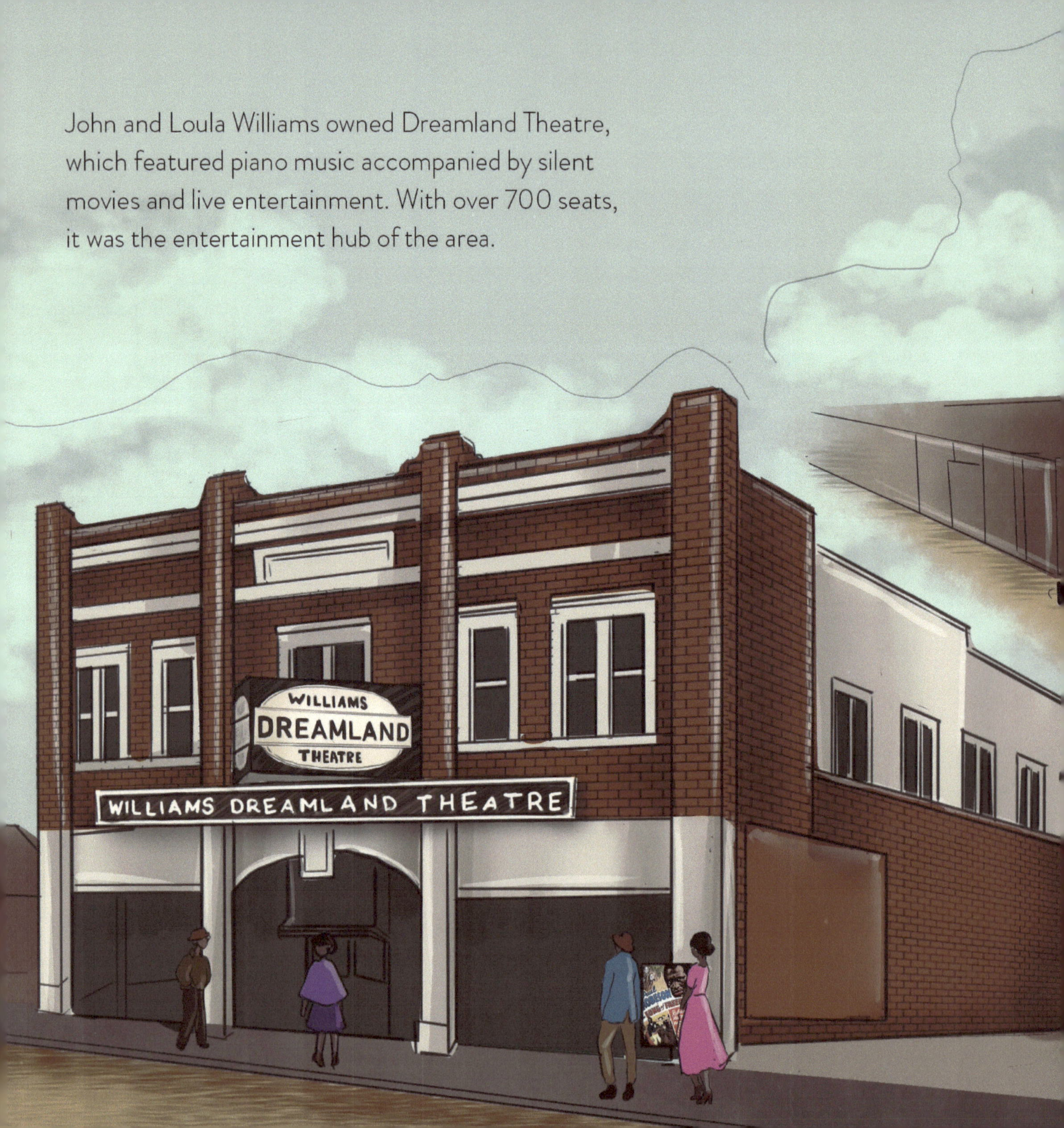

J. B. Stradford owned several rental properties, however his hotel was the highlight of the district. The Stradford Hotel was grand, with 54 guest rooms. It was considered the finest Black-owned hotel in the country. Gorgeous chandeliers hung from the ceilings in the lobby and in the banquet room. The hotel featured a pool room, a dining hall, and a salon for the guests' enjoyment.

These businesses were thriving, however, this would change on May 30, 1921, when two teenagers working downtown crossed paths. On that Memorial Day, D. Rowland, a Black boy who shined shoes, and Sarah Page, a white girl who operated elevators, had a fateful interaction in an elevator at the Drexel Building.

While alone in the elevator, the cable cart jerked, causing Rowland to accidentally step on Sarah's foot. Sarah reacted by slapping Rowland once. When she attempted to slap him a second time, he blocked her actions before she could hit his face. Sarah screamed and a nearby store clerk came to her aid. Fearing for his safety, Rowland ran away, and the store clerk called the police. The next morning, Rowland was arrested without being told what he was accused of doing.

When questioned by the police, Sarah told the officers that what happened in the elevator was an accident and that Rowland did not harm her. However, it was too late. A white-owned newspaper had already circulated rumors throughout the white community that Sarah had been harmed. This prompted an angry mob to gather outside the courthouse, wanting to harm Rowland.

In response, a group of Black men from the community went to the courthouse to support Sheriff Willard McCullough and help protect Rowland.

As the numbers grew on both sides, it was only a matter of time before conflict would erupt.

A gunshot was fired, and a fight began between the two groups.

The fighting continued throughout the Greenwood District. The small group of Black men were overwhelmed by the growing number of white men threatening their community.

These white men wanted to destroy the neighborhood. They stormed through the community, burning businesses and homes to the ground and harming anyone in their path.

Privately-owned planes circled the air and dropped makeshift bombs made of fabric soaked in turpentine. The pilots lit the bombs with matches before dropping them on properties in Greenwood, which reduced the buildings to rubble.

The attack caused the destruction of 35 blocks of the area known as Black Wall Street. More than 1,250 houses were burned, and 200 others were looted of valuables, including cash and family heirlooms such as jewelry.

Newspaper stations, schools, grocery stores, churches, hotels, and many other Black-owned businesses were destroyed or damaged by fire.

300 Black men, women and children were killed.

10,000 Black people were left homeless.

This community of entrepreneurs and homeowners suffered $50 – 100 million in property damage (which is equal to $660 million – 1 billion in today's value).

It took 15 years to build this blooming community, and within 48 hours, it was burnt to the ground.

However, out of the ashes, the community gathered to rebuild Black Wall Street. Although spirits were broken, and government help was limited, the small community that remained forced itself to move forward.

Archer ST 500
N Greenwood AV 100

Greenwood residents were resilient and determined, and they challenged city laws that made it difficult to rebuild on their own land.

Four years later, by 1925, this community was restored with the help from organizations such as the National Association for the Advancement of Colored People (NAACP); however the community was never the same.

From the shadows of Black Wall Street, other Black owned communities were able to grow and flourish.

OAKLAND

Where is the next Black Wall Street?

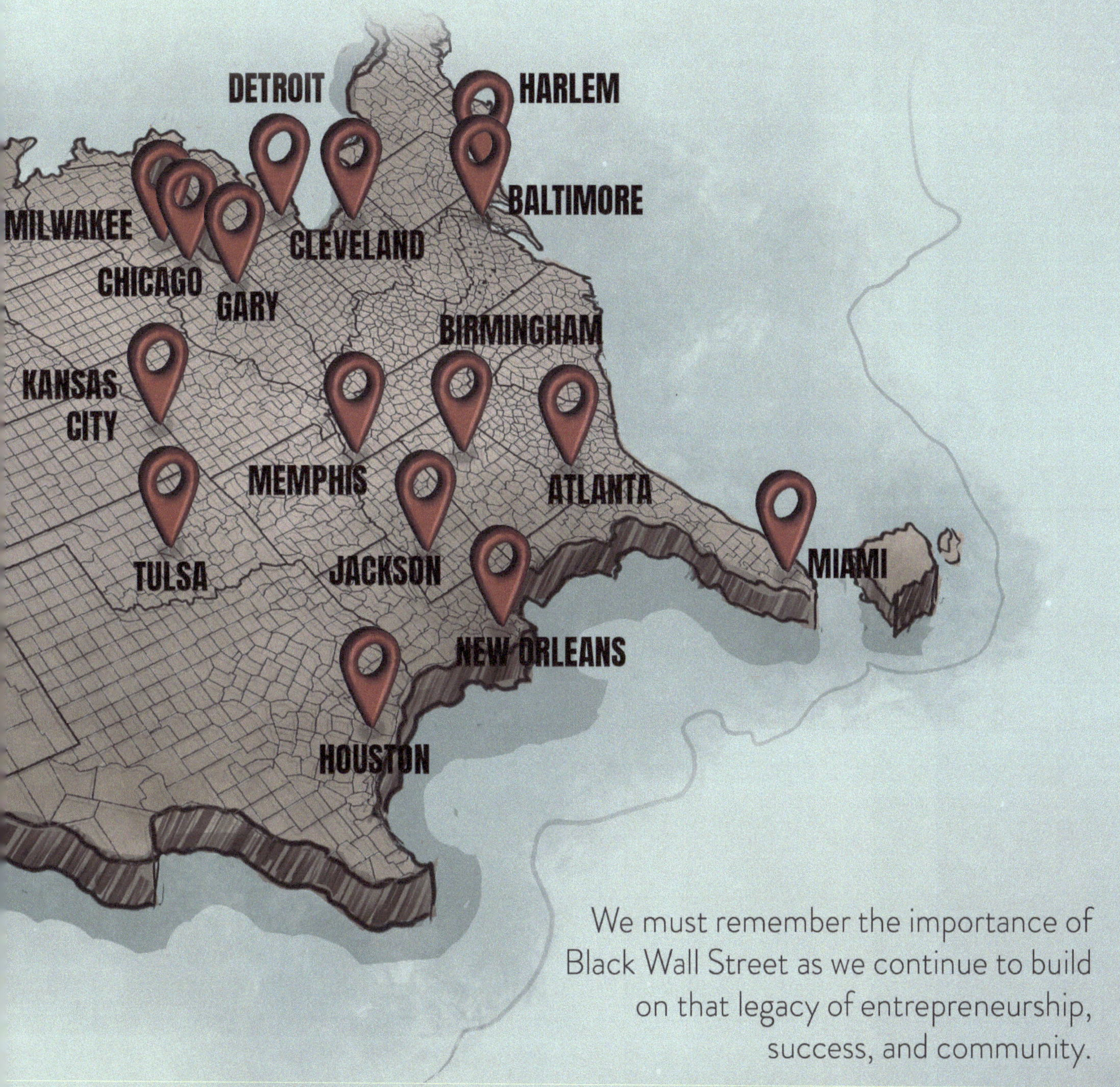

We must remember the importance of Black Wall Street as we continue to build on that legacy of entrepreneurship, success, and community.

McGowan
VARIETY STORE
CAVER'S CLEANING
OKLA EAGLE
DRUGS
WILLIAMS
SPANNS RECREATION
BLACK WALL STREET
Archer
N Greenwood

About the Author

LaQuitta Barnes is a former Title 1 reading teacher with over thirteen years of experience teaching scholars within the public school system in Houston, TX. She is passionate about exposing scholars to culturally inclusive resources that help inspire and challenge them to make rich textual connections. Through the years she served in various capacities such as Literacy Coach, District Mentor and Campus Administrator and was awarded campus Instructional Coach of the Year. As a versatile educator, LaQuitta has enjoyed transforming children's lives through literature and reshaping their future. She was inspired to write Black Wall Street: The Spirit of Community because of the lack of age-appropriate text to teach notable moments in history such as this amazing story.

Entrepreneurship is also close to her heart, for the past fourteen years she has found success as a licensed realtor and real estate investor. The rich history of Black Wall Street resonates with her family's goal of promoting the importance of entrepreneurship and generational wealth. Along with her husband and two children, LaQuitta has a passion for revitalizing her hometown by providing quality homes and creating a stronger sense of community. For more information and additional resources, please visit ***www.ourhistorytold.com.***

Glossary

Conflict - a fight, battle or struggle

Entrepreneur - a person who organizes and manages a business

Financial - relating to money

Heirloom - a valuable object that is owned by a family for many years and passed from one generation to another

Institution - an established organization

Migrant - a person who moves from one place to another, especially in order to find work or better living conditions.

Mob - a crowd bent on or engaged in lawless violence

Resilient - able to become strong, healthy, or successful again after something bad happens

Turpentine - a type of oil with a strong smell that is flammable

www.ingramcontent.com/pod-product-compliance
Lightning Source LLC
LaVergne TN
LVHW070159110826
845147LV00002B/448
9781736940617